Borrowed Magic

borrowed magic, Volume 1

william stone greenhill

Published by william stone greenhill, 2019.

BORROWED MAGIC

First edition. December 13, 2019.

ISBN: 978-1393721178

Written by william stone greenhill.

Borrowed Magic
And the Time We Ran Away from Sydney and Into a Haunted Forest

In the old times, magic ruled the world. Angels were the most prominent magical creature. But all was not well. Humans were being struck down and segregated by the magical. Because humans didn't have magic, they were suffering. But, 1000 years ago, a human Mage discovered new magic. Borrowed magic. No one remembers this Mage. People argue about their inspiration and methods of making the first borrowed artifact. But this human placed a magical creature extremity inside a gemstone to create a Borrowed Artifact and unleashed... borrowed power. This artifact would allow for humans to channel magic power through their bodies to fight back against their oppressors. Hundreds of years passed and borrowed magic became more and more prominent. But... the Angels created the first curse. A terrible new kind of magic that would punish humans. They thought themselves immune for they had magic inside them. They thought wrong.

I was in the Castle of Sydney. I arrived there last night. All the great kingdoms of Australia were gathering to sign a magical contract. I am from Perth, where I'm from, kids in Perth use what is known as borrowed magic. I arrived last night. Even the angels have been given safe passage into Sydney. Let's just say humans and angels don't get along. I am standing on the battlements of Sydney Castle. One of the three council members of Sydney said "you know Ethos, this contract will create a new age of peace, between humans and magical creatures. If this borrowed artifact works like Lord Mage Thunder says it will, the main political and magical powers won't be physically able to attack each other. It is imperative for the new generation to leave the mistakes of the past, in the past. I learnt that from your mother, Council Member Jane. She is a wise one, she owes it to many mistakes". All of a sudden, shadows emerged from the clouds. My mum stated "Ethos, find your sister. We must greet the Angels". I replied, "I'm coming". I ran into the guest room. I replied "Maggi, Maggi... are you hiding from me? Come on, we have to greet the angels". Every passing day more and more Darkling's are being born. Half angel half human creatures. They were becoming more common with every passing generation. I queried "Maggi, I know you're, in here. Damn it. She's not in here is she?". I looked at the window. It was open. I knew what that meant. I poked my head out only to see another open window down a few story's. There was a rope made of bed sheets descending down. I took the stairs down to the kitchen. Maggi was hiding underneath the table. I whispered "Maggi, this way now". She grabbed a pan full of brownies and yelled "come on, let's go". The cook walked in the door. He replied "you better not be stealing my cooking. Wait" sniff, sniff "you stole my brownies. Come back here". We bolted away through the castle corridors. I replied, "I'm all for stealing food from the kitchen, but what do we do about the angry cook?". He yelled "come back here". Maggi yelled "help, the cook is attacking me". A guard ran at him screaming "HALT ASASSIN". I replied, "he's not an assassin, he's just a disgruntled cook". The guards dragged him off. The guard replied "cook or not, we are under strict orders to keep the guests safe. He was charging at one of the contract signatories children. Such an act is punishable". We looked at the cook blankly, he was yelling and screaming and spitting. He bellowed "look for a loogie in your sandwich Look for a loogie in your sandwich". I asked, "does he want his brownie back?". We made our way to the Sydney Harbour Bridge. The Angels were landing on it one by one. There were only 7 angels from the West, 9 from the East, 6 from the South and 12 from the North. My mother approached the head Angel of the West, Fury. Fury replied, "this is my 56-year-old daughter Ava". I queried "um, she only looks about 11 maybe 12". Ava answered "in your years that would be correct, mortal. I see you have no... stolen power". My mum replied "I see time has done little to soften your grief. I assure you it has done little to soften mine". Fury spoke "as the younglings are saying in modern times, the past is the past". Maggi asked, "what are they talking about?". Me and Ava both said in unison "I'll tell you later". The angels of the south approached us. The young boy with a red mohawk and a spear yelled "I am Rellik, The Human Slayer. I've slayed Mage after Mage after Mortal. If this goes through, I won't be able to slay mortals anymore, but my dad said if I don't... he'll make my sister heir to the Angelic Western Throne. Can't have that can I?". The eastern Angel introduced herself "hello, I am Angelica. My family are the greatest magical power in the east of the continent. There aren't many left of us thanks to human poaching. This is my acquaintance, Ruby. She is the ruler of the Eastern Angelic Throne". The northern angel replied "I am Harbord. Ruler of the Northern Angelic Throne. If you'll excuse me, I have to go to the little lord's room". I pointed him in the right direction. Soon after we were in our quarters. Day had turned into night. Tomorrow night, the full moon would rise. And with it, humans would have the ability to create a borrowed artifact. Before borrowed artefacts humans were second class citizens. Some angels stood up for us, but they were in the minority. Humans don't have magic inside them. But, 1000 years ago, on the full moon, the first human mage found new magic. Borrowed magic. They sealed a sample from a magical creature inside a gemstone casing on the full moon to create borrowed magic. Within just over a century, humans were no longer victimized. But the angels were angrier than ever.

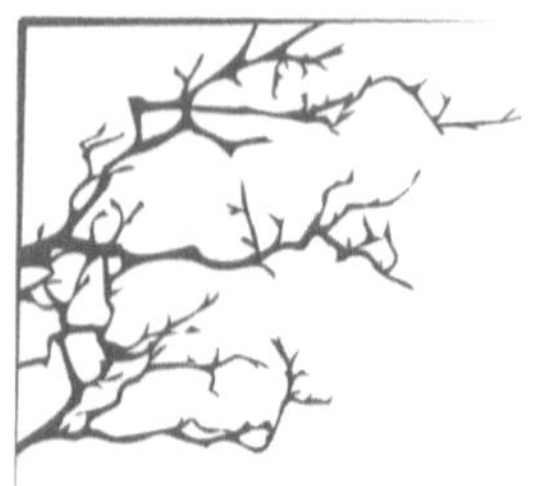

Chapter 2

Spirits Doom

Lightning woke me that night. There was a terrible storm. Maggi asked "Ethos, what did mum mean by, grief?". I replied, "that is a long story". Maggi responded "I've got time. I've been awake all night". I explained "well, a long time ago, our mum met a Cursed Angel in the forest. She was terrorising a village....." The door burst open with a rush of wind and lightning. Ava answered "tell the story right, boy. Your mother killed my sister". Maggi stammered with shock "you're lying. She would never do that. Never". I sighed "unfortunately, she isn't lying". Ava replied "I'm sorry, I didn't mean to scare you. I've just been through a lot, at the hands of this feud. It all started a decade ago before you were even born. Your mum had to go through military training to qualify for a spot on the council. She was patrolling a village one night. There had been reports of a Cursed Angel on the loose wreaking havoc. Unfortunately, my sister was also sent do deal with the problem". I took over "she walked into the local inn. She saw a man with a crystal wand in one corner. Jane walked up to him. He said, "it's a long way out from Perth for a guardian to be, isn't it?". The entire reception room turned their face toward her. she replied, "I'm here to deal with your... cursed problem". He warned "it's a bit much for a newbie guardian. How long have you been part of the council guard? A few weeks, a month or two?". She told him "umm, this is my first mission". He replied "Well, well, well it's not very often a daughter of a council member comes to a rundown place like this. My advice, turn back girl. Both angels and knights with considerable experience have come down here to face the Cursed Angel. None have prevailed. It will probably target you it will know you're here. Every night an angel from the woods turns into a shadow like phantom and takes trophies from the people. To make it even more terrifying, it's not like the council have been ignoring this problem. Run girl, run hard, run far". She replied "I'm sorry but if I turn down too many missions I will lose my right to be on the council. You understand". The mage said "very well, I'll show you your room. I just hope that the future council puts people above power. Jane said, "I do".

Back in the bedroom Maggi is hiding under the sheets listening intently. Ava interrupted "I'll take the next bit of the story. That night while your mum slept, my sister crept into her room. She sensed the cursed hiding in her closet. But the mage did not warn her that Spirit (my sisters name) was also in town. She approached the closet and your mother Jane awoke quietly. She grabbed her cross bow and aimed it at my sister. The creature smashed through the door and slammed into Spirit". I took over the story Spirit screamed "take the shot, take the shot, take the shot". And she did, but she hit the wrong person. But before Spirit died, she crushed a crystal in her hands and slammed it into the cursed back. The cursed was cured". Maggi stammered "wow, I never knew". I replied "and mum made me promise to never tell you what she did. So, let's never speak of it around her". Ava responded "people have died in this feud. And all in the name of magic. Whether it's borrowed, stolen, inherited, born, cursed or otherwise". Ava walked out.

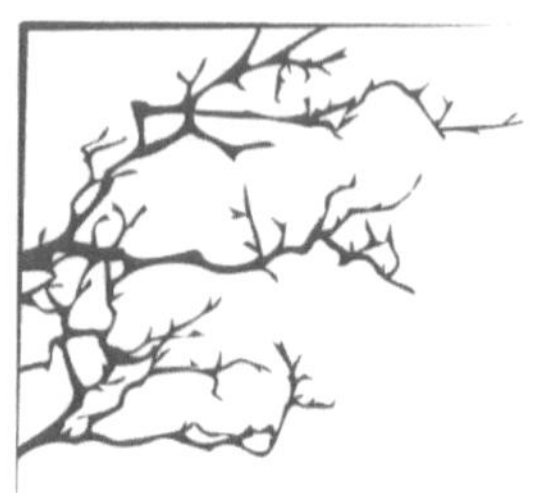

Chapter 3

Guards, Guard's and Night Angels

It was pitch black at 4:AM in the morning. It was a relatively peaceful night for a night so stormy but that doesn't mean dark forces weren't gathering. A guard named Jeremy was walking with his patrol buddy Jeremiah. Jeremy was a rather average father. He had a wife, 3 kids and liked to play golf on the weekends. His kids are named "Bill, Jill and Julie. Bill who was the only boy of the group likes to sew action figures. Julie and Jill like to create borrowed artefacts. You should see their faces light up when they finish a masterpiece. Jeremy and his wife Sue met at a doughnut shop and have loved doughnut's ever since. They enjoy Friday morning when they walk down to the local bakers to buy a family pack of doughnuts to bring them home for breakfast. The forest outside Sydney Castle was crawling with both creatures of Eastern and Southern magic. Mages were lucky to be able to use borrowed artefacts from creatures of both south and east. Unfortunately, powers from west and north weren't so common. Jeremy asked his partner "did you hear that? I think there is something in the bushes". Jeremiah replied "let me let you in on a little secret. the reason that patrols like this are given to cruddy guards like us is because nothing ever happens. Remember last night, when you thought a kangaroo was a cursed?". Jeremy replied, "that was a kangaroo but". Jeramiah interrupted "or the week before that when you thought there were mermaids in that river? Or your first week of patrol when you thought that bird was an angel? My point is guards like us get assigned to the areas were nothing ever happens. So, don't worry, nothing is ever going to happen". Jeremy replied as he walked further into the woods "I still have to check it out. It's my duty to the people inside that castle". Jeramiah yelled "what makes you think this will be any different than the last hundred times". Jeremy bellowed back through the brush "the peace treaty signing for one. Future of the nation at stake. Millions of powerful people want to wipe out the other side. Thousands of them are willing to do something about it". Jeramiah was an experienced guard. He showed promise in combat training and had decades of experience under his belt. But it was those decades that made him not the best guard. He started in the low risk areas like Jeremy did but he got comfortable with those areas. Complacent. Over time he was the go to training guard for young guards because of his will to stay in the low risk zones. The less danger happened, the more complacent he became. It was the cycle that was always going to be his downfall. He didn't even take his sword most nights. Jeremy wandered into the woods. He cleverly doused his torch so not to give away his position. A group of 8 not people stood above him in the trees. Jeremy saw them but pretended not to. He could call for help from his senior officer, but that would probably trigger them into reacting. Putting them both in danger. He could probably shoot a cursed arrow taking care of one but them another one would kill him. Jeremy didn't care for unnecessary spilt blood. He could keep walking and not let them know he knew they were there. On that hand he could show them his guard's badge and pull rank on them. If he let them know he knew they were there he would likely die were he stood. His best option as he decided was to buy time until he could find a battle-field where he would have an advantage. It was stupid, they were 8 of them and the nearest guards would take 5 maybe 6 minutes to get there. Then, another option occurred to him. Fire an emergency flare and guards would rush inti the area. But he would die before they got there. Then he saw a cliff. He remembered a conversation from the dressing room that there was a party in the waters just over that cliff. Jeremy walked ever closer to the cliff. But when he saw the leader woman of the Angel's hand signal "kill the senior guard" Jeremys heart rate increased. An expression of worry crept onto his face. He wanted to run to save Jeramiah but he knew that would put them both in danger. He would have to hope that Jeramiah could take care of himself. He heard a younger angel say "he knows we're here. Kill on my mark". Jeremy bolted. He bolted like his life depended on it because it did. You don't know what you can do until you're faced with death. The answer will always surprise you. He heard his mentor scream in pain. "WAHHHH" Jeremy reflected "it's horrible, but with his attitude... inevitable". Jeremy bolted through the small path and before he could jump into the river, he slammed into an invisible wall. A young girl, an angel who would only be about 60 something which is 13 in our years pinned Jeremy against the wall. All his work, the moths of training... had they done nothing for him. The only thing he had found remotely useful in his training was the talk at lunch. Then Jeremy saw something. A necklace made of moon stone with a feather inside it". Jeremy stalled for time "I know you want to kill me, but I have three kids. Please. Wait, that necklace... it's a borrowed artefact. But angels can't use those". She readied an attack at his upper head using the borrowed necklace. If he could snatch it even for a second, it would break the wall and he could jump. "angels despise humans borrowing their power. Angels borrowing power is considered an atrocity. What does it feel like, to be hated by both humans... and your own". She got distracted for about half a second. The guard grabbed the borrowed necklace and jumped over the side. While he was falling, he fired a flare into the air.

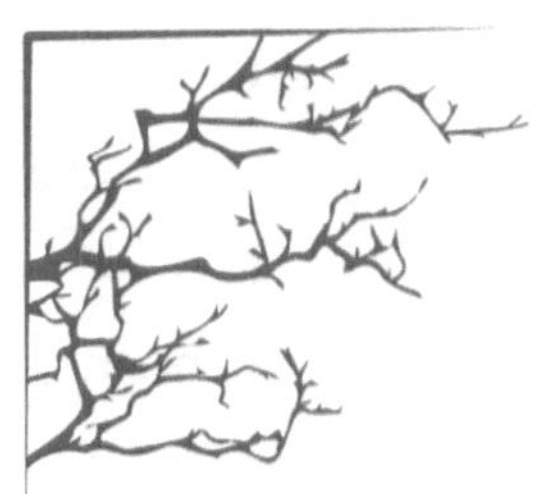

Chapter 4

We Get Up for Snacks

It was late at night and Jeremy ran into the castle. He woke a sleeping High Spell (head magic user for a kingdom) of the town. The middle-aged woman yelled "what is the meaning of this intrusion". Jeremy yelped "ma'am, it is in the guards hand-book under "so you've been attacked by an Angel" sub section B, article 6, paragraph 5. All guards that get attacked by an angelic force and live, are to report it to the strongest spell caster of their respective City. In this case that is you, ma'am". The woman got up and studied Jeremy she said "you have been in a scuffle with an angelic assassin? You have done your capital well but.... Jeremy blurted out "they were using borrowed magic Ma'am". She asked "what did they look like. What colour were their wings? Tell me boy". Jeremy replied, "black as night with wild purple eyes". The high mage yelled "focus. Are you sure they were using borrowed power? Absolutely sure?". Jeremy stammered "I could never forget that face. I recovered this from the Angel ma'am". He gave her the borrowed artefact. She stammered "they sound like night Angel's, but I need to be sure. I'll have to do some research on this artefact but in the meantime, how on magic's earth did you manage to recover a borrowed artefact from an angel?". The boy said "I just jumped off a cliff ma'am" like he was asking a question. The mage said "I would expect no less from a lord mage. I would expect a promotion within the month boy, but for now... wake the council members, tell the guards to be on high alert and I'll wake the high angels. Do not rouse the children of the mages. Am I clear? Those kids have enough to worry about". Jeremy ordered "at once ma'am. If one of the council members asks why they need to be awake what should I tell them?". The High Spell ordered "don't call me ma'am. I am Joy Thunder of Sydney. Oh, and one more thing, wake my daughter lucky. She came in from Perth last night after living with her father for 9 years. I will need her help researching this artefact. Oh, and one last thing, this is need to know only. I don't want a panic". "yes, Joy of Sydney" finished Jeremy. He ran off to tell the lords. Meanwhile, I awoke again to Maggi's stomach growling. she replied, "I am so hungry". Ethos said "come on, let's find some food. I need a glass of water anyway my throat is killing me". We got out of bed and walked into the hallway. We had almost made it to the library when we ran into a familiar face. I asked "Lucky? What are you doing up at 4:20AM?". She answered "umm, what are you doing up?". Maggi replied, "getting food and water. What are you doing up?". She answered, "doing research for a class project". I queried "they wouldn't give you a class project on a day like today. Not when the fate of the world is hanging in the balance. And your studying curses, those books are about angelic breeds and borrowed artefacts". "see ya", she said as she sped off". Maggi asked "I wonder what the adults are keeping from us? Wanna threaten to push one of them off the astronomy tower if they don't tell us?". I yelled "no". "You take all the fun out of things" said Maggi. Maggi sighed "you take all the fun out of things. You do know that she was cursed with the bad luck curse?". A ladder fell on her. "if you get near her bad luck will rub off on you". I replied, "she's an out-cast Maggi, for that exact reason". Maggi replied, "we're totally following her, aren't we?". "Yep".

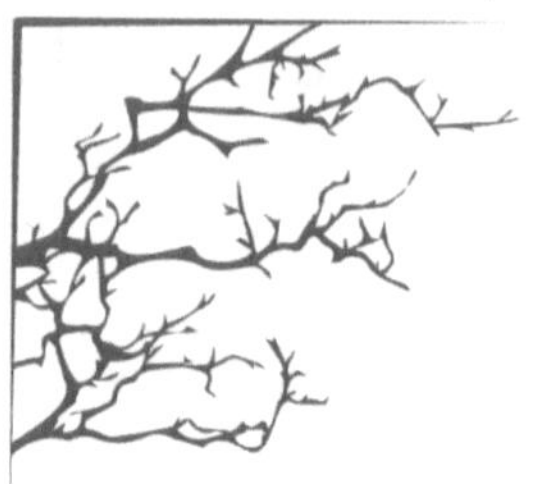

Chapter 5

We Hide in a Closet

We found ourselves in a corridor following Lucky. I whispered "are you sure this will work? What are the odds of her slipping on a marble?". Maggi replied, "with a luck curse on her, pretty high". Maggi rolled the marble around the corner and before she could walk into the door of her study, she tripped. Unluckily for her, there was a wet floor down an interlocking hallway. She tripped and slid down the hall. She was 20 meters down the hall when we rushed inside the door. I motioned "quickly, in the closet". We hid in with a bunch of dress robes. Ava was already in the closet. Maggi whispered, "what are you doing here?". Ava answered "the same as you. Finding out what they are keeping from us. Lucky walked into the room. Her mother walked in shortly after. She was carrying a necklace. She asked "I need your expert opinion. This locket was taken from an angel. Apparently an Angel that can use... borrowed magic. I need to know for sure what clan it belongs to". Lucky asked "any idea what direction the angel was born in? That could be the key to finding it". "None" said Thunder "but if you study the engraving it says O.S.N. I think that may mean Order of the Sleepless Night. A group of rogue Night Angels who specialise in borrowed magic and human curses. They are the exact people who would stop the peace. They believe rogue angels like them will never be free if the current angelic rulers have their way. And without the humans to pose a threat to the angelic kingdoms... They would believe that would be the final nail in the coffin". Lucky looked up the Order of the Sleepless Night and found "yep, according to at least three of the texts this belongs to them. And it is definitely angelic craftsmanship. Whether it was stolen from one of them and used by another rogue angel is another matter entirely". Thunder stated "that is enough information to bring to the council members and the angelic lords. The aboriginal tribes should be arriving today along with the last capital. Adelaide, the cursed city. The only major human city that accepts cursed beings openly".

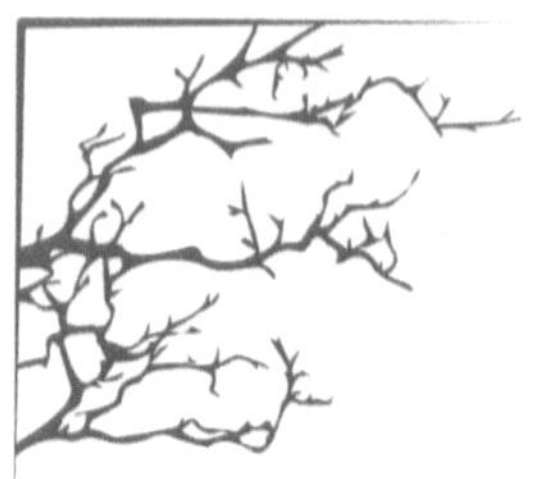

Chapter 6

Moon Rise

They day passed rather normally. Well, as normal as a day in Sydney Castle can go. Especially for a world changing day. The aboriginal elders and the three children of the council of Adelaide arrived. The Sydney council welcomed them with open arms. Eventually sun set was only an hour from occurring. That is when things got interesting. Ava was walking through the hall casually. She was headed to the banquet where they were holding the creation of the borrowed artefact slash binding magical contract. Me and my sister Maggi were hiding in the walls. Ava realized that someone was following her and cried "show yourself. I know you're there". She waited for 10 minutes and still nothing. Finally the words "give me your memory" sounded through the empty corridor. A flash of purple light rushed down the corridor and split into two precise beams hitting Ava in the temples. She screamed and passed out for 5, maybe 6 minutes. In that time the attacker, a female angel about her age, took her into a closet and dressed her in one of their uniforms. She also gave her a number of borrowed artefacts. She replied as Ava awoke "Sleepless Angel Ava, I have your orders. You must find and terminate Jane Reeper and her two children. Ethos and Maggi. I have already done my job so I will meet you outside. May the Will of the Borrowed be with you". Ava walked out of the closet. Meanwhile, I was hiding in the walls with my little sister. I asked "Maggi, do you really think that hiding in the walls is better than the banquet? I mean it's the most guarded place in the castle". Maggi responded "those guys are goners. The guards will act as a map straight to them. We've already given our hair for the artefact. And this way we can spy on people. If my intuition is correct, the banquet hall should be around here". We peeked out of the portrait hole. We saw things we didn't need to see. There were guards changing out of there armour. I turned around and dry retched. "do not look in there". Maggi asked, "what did you see?". I replied, "not something for kid's eyes". Maggi queried "but you're a kid?". I answered "I know, and damnit... I don't want to see that again". We continued this time under my leadership. I replied "from memory, the banquet hall has a shower near it. Probably because all the guests rooms are in that wing of the castle. So, if we follow the hot water pipes which are connected to a geyser in the outside forest, we should find them. We approached the banquet hall. We stuck our eyes through the one-way painting and saw the banquet. A shadowy figure moved in the distance. I looked through the portrait hole and saw a brawl. But that shouldn't have been possible. Either the contract hadn't been signed yet or, I shuddered to think, the contract hadn't worked, and war was on the horizon. I rushed to down the hall. I got a feeling, I yelled "Maggi, in here... now. I pressed the gemstones on the floor. They were in a pattern on the floor. Amethyst Rose Quartz, Clear Quartz, Smoky Quartz. The floor opened into a staircase. We walked into the room. We quickly shut the door behind us. Just then, the door opened. We were in a study with notes beyond imagining. There were maps and artefacts beyond human description. There were spell books with curses that never existed before. There were powers impossible and the place was filled with maps. Maggi stammered "I could go a life-time studying this. Where is this place?". Ava walked down the stairs dressed in O.S.N clothes. She threatened "The Order of the Sleepless has been looking for you. You should say hello to your mother for me". Meanwhile half an hour ago, the banquet was about to begin.

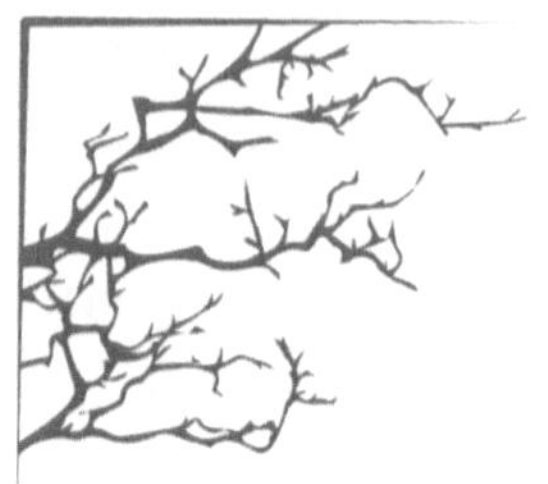

Chapter 7

The Brawl at the Banquet

The banquet had begun approximately half an hour ago. The crowd was getting rowdy. Rellik, the heir to the Southern Angelic throne had a few glasses of ale. And, by a few, I mean 8. Lucky walked up to him and asked "umm, are you sure you should be having that. This is a peace treaty". Rellik blabbered "I'll do what I want. I'm a bloody prince, Angel". Thunder told lucky telepathically "don't worry, I had the chef burn off the alcohol. I cast a spell on it to make it taste like the real thing". Lucky thought back "wait, if its fake, how come the crowd is getting rowdy. Rellik is acting really stupid and so are the others". Thunder responded "I don't know. I guess it's some kind of placebo effect". Thunder was talking to my mother Jane. She asked "this is a new day for us all. I just wish the Angelic Lords and the Council Members would take this more seriously". An angel walked up to Thunder. She replied "I have a feather from the Ruby family. The greatest angelic magical power in the east". Thunder gave it to her two assistants Julie and Jill. They took a triangular piece of crystal and placed a special tree sap based glue on it. They put the feather onto the triangles they had already put together. They placed the triangle on top of the feather and gently pressed them together. It had hardened into the rest of the triangles. Thunder answered "I have been sensing an angel outside. It is a hostile presence. Wait, you're going after it, aren't you?". Jane walked toward the door. Thunder said "at least be careful. We don't know what this thing is". My mum walked away from the banquet and into the halls. She eventually came to a darkened figure. We cut to a scene outside. "Oh, it's you" my mum said. "wait, what are you doing? Stop! I won't do it again. I won't kill again. Never again". She refused to strike a lethal blow as she was ruthlessly cut down. Flashes of light erupted from the window. Jane eventually lay on the floor bleeding. Lucky walked behind her in the hallway. She was dying She ran up to her and screamed "how could you do this? Ok, focus, healing spells. Healing spells". Jane muttered "too late. Protect, Maggi". Lucky stammered "I won't let this happen Aunty Jane. Ok, how do I do this?". She chanted "by the power of the destructive lie send my face into the sky" and a face erupted from her borrowed artefact. The message was sent to the medical healers. She took off Janes hair and stammered "there is only one thing I know how to do that might save her". she took the gemstone from a stone someone had dropped. She used magic to cut open the stone then heat it. She took a lock of my mother's hair to make a borrowed artefact. Meanwhile at the banquet Thunder bellowed "everyone, I have finished the artefact. It will hence forth be known as the Key of Harmony. If it works, you won't be able to hit each other. But more importantly, you won't be able to wage war against one another. Nor will any future family you may have. This is a tremendous accomplishment. Intelligent life has come together to do something extraordinarily rare. Work together for the greater good. But before we celebrate, we need to test it. And before we do that, I need to tell you that isn't real alcohol you're drinking. It was a placebo effect". Most of the people who chose to be immature sobered up pretty fast. except for Rellik and Harbord who didn't know what a placebo was. Harbord yelled in a drunken slur "how are we meant to do that?". Thunder answered "punch someone. It is the only way to test it". Rellik punched Harbord. It hit him square on. Angelica shot a paralysis spell at the council member of Darwin. Followed by Fury attacking Rellik head on. The council of Adelaide got into a fist fight with the council of Hobart who was already was fighting the head eastern angel Fury. It became a brawl. Did you ever wonder why they call Thunder, Thunder? It's because when she casts a spell it shakes the heaven's and the earth. Thunder slammed her foot against the ground screaming "Power of thunder hear my cry. Use my power this feud must die!". With that stomp a bang big enough to crack the Castle sending waves of destructive sound and shooting sparks all over the castle. The very earth and sky shuddered with her power and everyone got knocked onto their butts. Thunder reasoned "now, we knew there was a chance this wouldn't work, so let's not act like toddlers and hit each other. There are three possibility's. One of the most likely is the Night Angels did something to mess with the artefact. It could be someone here sabotaged the contract on purpose". The heir to the council of Adelaide yelled "it was Rellik. That guy has hunted my family for..." Thunder yelled "QUIET! We need to keep our heads. If we go pointing fingers there is going to be a war bigger than any we have ever seen. Angels will descend from the clouds. Humans will shoot flaming balls of destruction into the clouds and hell on earth will begin. The native humans will flood into the capital cities and the clouds alike with their borrowed power. Millions of lives will be lost before we do what we were always going to do. Sit and talk. The final option is by far the most likely. People didn't enter this agreement with their full heart and mind. Those who selflessly agreed will be protected from the rest while those who didn't agree will be fair game". Rellik yelled "if there's going to be a war, I'll kill you all right here. Then there will be no war". Thunder threatened "if you do that, I swear on magic itself I will bring the roof down on all of you and every non protected party and squash you like bugs. I suggest that we all leave, Now!". Everyone left but the tensions between the governments of Australia were higher than ever.

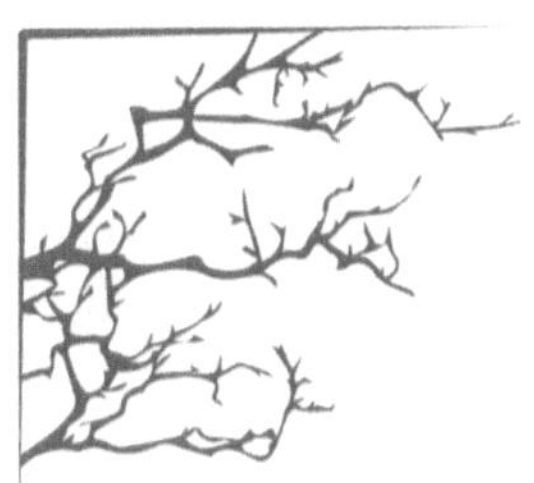

Chapter 8

Ethos Becomes a Mage

Ava walked into the room as Ethos grabs a borrowed artefact. Ava replied, "try anything you want it still won't save you". Ethos noticed Ava's dilated pupils. Maggi screamed "what do you mean, say hello to our mother for you? You were working for them all along. You can probably use borrowed artefacts just like them too. Was that noble "I hate all magic" thing just an act?". Ava stammered "what do you mean, I hate all magic? I literally have never said that". Ethos queried "you seriously just said that this morning". She spoke jittering "enough of your mind games. If you get your way, borrowing angels will never have their rights". I realized "wait a minute? Erratic behaviour, dilated pupils... isn't that two of the sign of a memory curse? I remember High Spell Crab telling me that. That was after a magic student had altered my memory". Ava screamed "I have not been brain washed. I am a Borrowing Night Angel". I looked at the stick I was holding. It was made of amethyst with a green hair in it. I queried "doesn't your sister have green hair... moss green hair?". Ava replied, "did your mum notice that while she was cutting her down?". I answered "I just have a feeling. An odd feeling. Like, I know this hair belongs to her. I can't explain it, but I just know". Maggi replied "if your right this could be big. As long as a borrowed artefact with the D.N.A of the deceased still exists. Human magic can bring them back to life". Maggi continued "curses always leave a physical mark on the body. Look at your temples. if your mind has been violated there will be marks on both of them". Ava yelled "enough lies". A flash of green light appeared on the artefact. Green light briefly showed on Ava's forehead and heart. She stammered "what happened? wait... what did I do? Oh god what did I do?". I yelled "focus Maggi. How do you bring a borrowed back to life?". Maggi replied "you need some very special magic. It has to come from the direction they were born in. You need a picture of the person you want to bring back to life and some kind of body". The staircase dropped down and Lucky fell onto her face. She was carrying more borrowed artefacts than an entire class of student mages. She screamed "you are going to pay... Ava". Lucky asked "for what?". I yelled "no, Lucky. She was under a spell". Lucky bellowed "you think I don't know that. After what she did, I don't care". Tears swelled up in Lucky's eyes. Ava dropped to her knees stammering about what she might have done. Lucky screamed "I summon frost" and threw a bolt of icy wind straight at the distracted Ava. I jumped in front of the icy wind thrusting the borrowed artefact at the cold attack. The attack curved into a concentrated beam of ice crystals which could have penetrated the castle walls. Meanwhile a council member of Sydney was having a shower in the upstairs bathroom. The attack of ice refracted bounced off the borrowed artefact containing Spirits hair and slammed into the ceiling. Unfortunately, the water pipes were on the ceiling. Lucky bellowed "out of the way Ethos. You don't know who you're protecting". But then the water pipe ruptured pouring hot water all over Lucky. Meanwhile upstairs in the shower the lady was In the middle of the shower. She was just about to grab a bar of soap when the water turned cold. She yelled "Ahh, ahh... what! Who turned off the heat?". The gang heard the screaming in the shower from upstairs. I screamed "RUN" as Maggi put a chain onto Lucky's arm. Lucky yelled through the hall "I won't let you escape. You monster". You should have seen the look of horror on Ava's face. She just wanted to shut down and cry. A borrowed artefact flew out of Lucky's hand and into mine. Lucky yelled from back in the room "Spirits of the wild. Hunt the Darkened Angel". We ran out of the tunnels. Angelic warriors, human guards and native warriors were fighting right front and centre. A student Borrowed Mage was clashing with 7 Sydney guards. Ava stated "that was good thinking. Borrowed magic can't destroy a borrowed artefact". I stammered "who the hell was thinking". They got knocked down with a massive shock wave going through the tiles. We ran past as ghostly wolves barrelled through the halls. We reached a door and Ava kicked it open. She struck one of the wolves with a scythe. But it just slashed through. We eventually reached the door. It would take time for the gate to open. Maggi stammered "Ava, you're an Angel. Do magic on those wolves". Ava yelled "do I look like a spell caster to you?". I looked at the orb in my hand for the first time. I saw a black hair in it. I screamed "bubble of the night" and put my hand to my mouth. I blew into it as I thrust my hand forward. A bubble the size of a chair and the ghost of the wild dog got trapped inside. Another dog popped it. Then a ghostly owl lunged for Ava's throat. I murmured "I summon frost" and cold wind blew all over everything around us. The ghostly creatures ran away from the cold. Harbord's angelic guard screamed "you there, Borrowed Spell Caster, open this door". I stammered "Spell Caster. I'm not a Spell Caster". He screamed "I just saw you do magic. Magic you stole from my kind. So, use it already". I thought to myself "wait... I did do magic. I DID MAGIC". The guard screamed "open the door you idiot". I stammered "umm, I only know three spells but... I summon frost". And ice froze the chains. Ava grabbed the guards arrow and shot the part of the chain I had frozen. The other chain holding the draw-bridge buckled and broke with the wait. It fell and we ran across. Ava yelled "I'm saving my sister. Any volunteers from here on out are free to leave at any time. I replied "of course I'm with you. But, I have to ask, what did you do to make Lucky that mad? She's not that kind of person. But whatever you did made her want to hurt you. Not just hurt you but want to make you suffer. What on magics earth did you do?". Ava stammered "I wish I knew. I can't remember anything from the moment I got mind wiped to the moment I woke up. It's all a haze with a few image's". Maggi replied "yeah, having your mind forcefully breached will do that to you. No telling what else is missing in your memory". We bolted to the cart we took from Perth. That cart had a mage using magic to push it forward at speeds a horse couldn't hope to go. Ava replied, "I can fly carrying you both to the West of the continent in a couple of days…". I interrupted "I may not know much about magic, but I know that any human city would shoot down an angel when there is this kind of tension in the air. Even if they were carrying two humans". Ava asked, "transportation spell?". Maggi answered "sorry, nope. The humans will be blocking angelic teleportation just like the angels will be blocking human teleportation". We hurried to the platoon of Perth carriages. Ava stammered "that's your plan. Get in the carriage and leave me behind". Maggi criticised "yeah big brother. That's a stupid plan". I replied "you don't get it. There is a compartment under the seat that we are meant to crawl into if things go wrong. Its more than big enough for Ava and we can hide her in it. This way may be risky but it's the least risky way we have. And the fastest without getting blown out of the sky or discombobulated. We could walk, but its Ava's choice. Quick and relatively risky, or slow and safe with the high probability of getting attacked by guards, assassins or cursed. Ava replied "relatively risky. And just like that, a couple of dozen guards from Canberra, Melbourne and Darwin charged us. The head guard said "we can decide which heir is taken hostage by who later. For now, we just capture them". Another guard screamed "KILL THE ANGEL. She is worthless to us and a potential threat. Focus all your fire power on the angel". I screamed "Spirits of the wild. Hunt the cowardly guards". Wild cats and birds of prey charged at the guards. They screamed "regroup, regroup". But arrows and magical lightning erupted from the castle battlements. Ava screamed "FOR THE WOODS" and we bolted into the trees in the blackness. We spent until 9:30 running away from guards wanting to take us hostage. And knights from Perth who wanted to save us but kill Ava. We eventually found ourselves in a secluded part of the woods inaccessible to anyone but an angel like Ava. We fell asleep under the light of the full moon. With the chaos that surrounded us a very real danger.

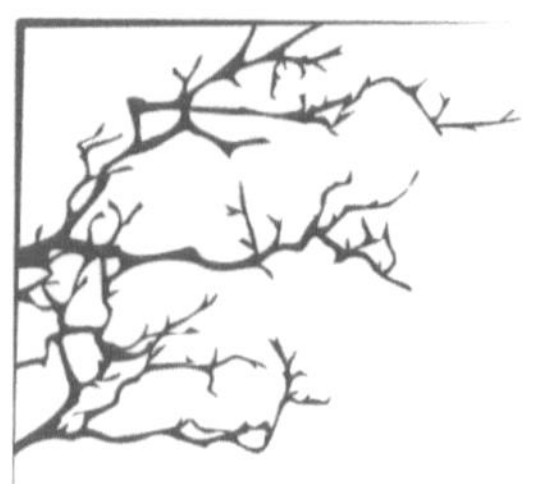

Chapter 9

Yin and Yang, the Lightning Struck Tower and the Shield.

It was early morning. Ava screamed in her sleep at 4:20AM. "NO, NO, DON'T DO IT. DON'T KILL HER NO. I WON'T, YOU CAN'T MAKE...... she awoke with a scream. I asked, "bad dream?", she replied "yeah, I have a feeling it's got something to do with that memory charm. Something I feel insanely guilty about. Can I ask you something?". I replied, "that depends if we're playing truth or dare". Ava queried "just listen, your name... why are you called Ethos?". I answered, "why are you called Ava?". She replied "that's not what I mean. Ethos is a heavily angelic name. it's just 1000 years ago when borrowed magic was new humans weren't allowed to name their kids any kind of angelic name. Angels had this list of names, names only angels were allowed to have. Ava, Able, Halloween, Fury and Ethos just to name a few. The parents could be locked in jail for the first few years of their kid's life for giving them an angel name. The thing is, when borrowed mages rebelled against the angelic lords they named their kids these names as a show of defiance. To say we don't care because you can't touch us anymore. This was especially relevant because names have power and angels took away that power. Technically humans did us a favour by discovering borrowed magic and rebelling. Because of this, angels governing systems became less rigid and more power went to the people. Now if the community disagrees with the Angelic Lord, they can call a vote against the decision. Despite what most angels think about borrowed power it did us a huge favour". I replied "I don't know why I'm called Ethos. It's kind of ironic since I wasn't meant to be a mage". Ava asked "Why? Do humans not let the children of their lords have magic?". Ethos replied, "no its just my prophecy". Ava looked at me like I was nuts. "you know, my prophecy. When a human child is born the parent's get a seer to look into their future. Lucky got the black cat, and the symbols for borrowed and cursed. Her signs point to being a powerful cursed unlucky spell caster, fluent in borrowed magic. Mine are a little bit more mysterious. Yin and Yang. That can mean anything from good and evil to moon and sun. The lightning struck tower and lastly, the shield. At least a mysterious birth prophecy makes a good conversation starter. The shield means valiant protector. Any kind of mortal weaponry normally means swash buckling hero. Unfortunately, mortal weaponry in a birth prophecy is almost a guarantee that you won't learn magic". Ava stammered "but, you did learn magic. And way too easily I might add. Normally even angels struggle to master magic and they remain student mages for just under a century. Extended life has a lot of benefits". I replied "we should probably look at our options. There are probably bounty hunters on the loose. Not to forget to mention cursed, Sydney guards, agents from other kingdoms, darkened angels, magical beasts and last but not least... booby traps both natural and made". Maggi replied "it's probably safer if we go in the morning. While it's still dark there will be less chance of guards catching us and despite the higher presence of cursed in the night there more likely to go after the higher amount of guards. And you know, cover of darkness. We wandered out of the woods. Eventually we found a poster that said

"reward for safe return to Perth. Two heirs from the council are missing. Look for Ethos Reeper and Maggi Reeper Reward: 50000 golden pieces.

Maggi: Short young girl with blond hair and blue eyes.

Ethos: 14-year-old non magical human. Long white hair, scrawny build, shortish, one blue and one green eye".

I stated "scrawny, scrawny... that's about accurate". Maggi simply said "your gunna need more borrowed artefacts".

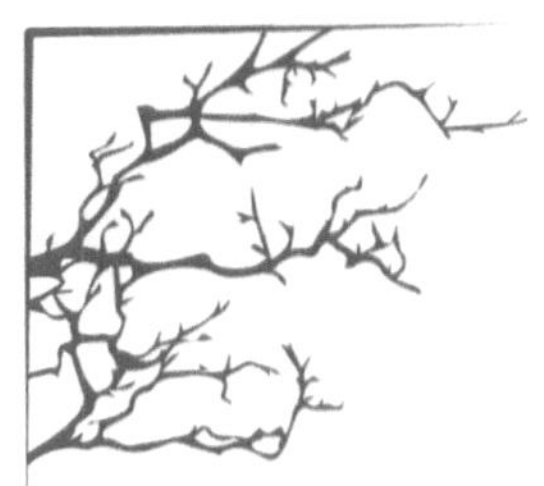

Chapter 10

The Muffin Mage

We are with Lucky back in the castle. High Spell Crab of Perth has just teleported there minutes before the angels cut off all Borrowed Magic transportation. Thunder explained "Crab is going to look for the two heirs to the Angelic Throne. Thankfully we agreed to an alliance with Sydney in exchange for locating the two heirs two The Council of Perth. They wanted an alliance with your father's side because the two heirs to Janes seat on the council are being protected by the Key of Harmony. And Perth wanted an alliance with Sydney because we have the key of harmony. As long as the key works, none of the high magical powers can attack Perth or those two kids. The same goes for anyone they tell to attack them. Even if the northern angels sent an army to attack them, they could just walk right through the ranks. Crabby will locate them and bring them back safe. You have a task just as important. Do you know of the Muffin Mage?". Lucky asked "The Muffin Mage owns a bakery. There is a sign on the door that says all who are accepting are welcome. He lets people in no matter their age, gender, species or race. He lets in cursed, magical and non-magical alike. He is also a gifted mage. Particularly fluent in transforming borrowed artefacts into the magical life forms they came from". Thunder replied "we need his help again. Jane is dead but the borrowed artefact you made can resurrect her".

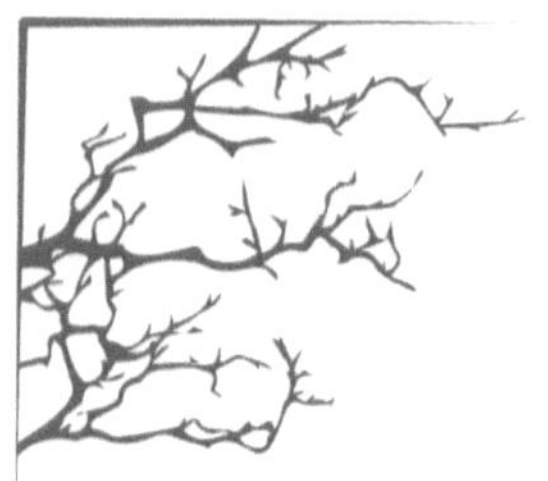

Chapter 11

How Can I Dump a Kingdom on My Sister?

I told Maggi while we were walking around the woods "I have been giving this a lot of thought and if this conflict takes our mother and older sister Ria, I want you to have the seat. I really want to learn magic and I can't do that if I'm bound with that kind of responsibility". Maggi asked "wait, why do I have to get a seat on the council? I have a life too. I don't want millions of people looking to me for wisdom. You're the oldest". I replied "hey, I was given power for a reason. I can't find that reason if I'm tied down with political responsibility". Maggi asked, "yeah but I know much, much more about magic than you". I asked "doesn't that make you the better choice? If you know more about magic and angelic culture, then you also know how to best combat the angels. You are also twice the strategist I am". Maggi replied "you have done military training. I haven't, that means I'm not eligible for a seat". Ava queried "wait, you're fighting over who doesn't rule the kingdom?". We both yelled "YES". Ava queried "isn't that a little weird. All throughout history siblings have clashed over power. Now two siblings are fighting to dump the responsibility on the other". We said in unison "damn straight". "you two are weird" Ava stated. A horse drawn carriage approached us. There was a chubby man on it with long sleeves, a bandana over his face, long comfortable pants, worn out leather boots and short black pig tails. He asked "good morning young travellers. I am a humble merchant. I'll be going as far as the next suburb. But that's as far as I'll be going today. They say there's a storm coming this week. You can hop in the back of the carriage if you want. I hear there are Perth guards on the loose. Searching for the heirs". We thought "what the hell" and hopped in the back with the veggies and live-stock. He took off at speeds that we couldn't have gone on foot. He asked "I bet thy be the heirs and their escort. Let me guess young lass, a Perth student mage who is accompanying the young council members back to Perth?". Ava replied "I'm an Angel, that's all you need to know. I've already said more than I should have". He asked "and you two, are the rumours true? People are saying that council member Jane is dead. I'm so sorry if its true". My heart sank. I stammered "I, I, I don't know if its true. I ho, hope it isn't". The guy replied "there is every chance this is a strategic ploy from Perth. Spread a rumour, have the other kingdoms think the council is in a moment of weakness and strike while people think you are weak". I replied "my turn, you are covering up most of your skin. I can see the slightest part of a black mark on your cheek above your bandana. I'm guessing you were recently cursed". He explained "you got me boyo. I was in the docks last week. I was in the markets when an angel cursed me and called me a thief". Maggi replied "yeah, angels call humans thieves a lot. They think we steal power from them to create Borrowed

Artefacts. But it's a matter of perspective. Some people say we steal power, some say we share it and others say we borrow it. Some even say that angels aren't using the power so their acting like children". The guy replied "yeah, the ironic thing is the angel didn't know how right she was. I am actually a thief. Ever heard of Fatso?". Maggi queried "the guy who tags the word Fatso at every location he steals from?". Fatso replied, "the very same". I yelled "Fatso stole a priceless family relic from the Reeper family. It is invaluable and irreplaceable. A relic from the days of the first borrowed mages. A journal made to promote the rise of the non-magical. One of the very few copies that still exist. Written by the first borrowed mage ever. they are rarer than diamonds and contain magic here to unheard of". He replied "oh, I'm sorry. Its in the back. I've kept it all this time. Every time I tried to sell it the buyer was an undercover operative trying to take me to Fremantle Prison. I've broken out of there 6 times and counting". Ava queried "Rellik said multiple times that he wants you dead. He told us that you stole a ceremonial sword. An ancient one". Fatso answered "ha, I stole a stuffed toy. A dog. He's been trying to kill me ever since. You know, if you want, I can show you the muffin mages card. I've been there before, and he helped me heal my cancer. He might be able to help you with whatever you're doing that's so classified". Maggi replied "I've heard of him. Isn't he that the baker who can turn borrowed artefacts into people. He is extremely fluent with that spell". Ava replied "I've been there. He hangs a sign on the door that says all who are accepting are welcome". I asked "can I send a message to my sister with this magpie messenger? Our family has been trying to get cursed accepted in Perth for 4 generations. This conflict might be the perfect opportunity for that". Fatso replied "sure, paper is in the back. If you can get my kind accepted in a major city, I'll gladly give you a piece of paper and a bird". Maggi queried "you stole this cart, didn't you?". "Absolutely".

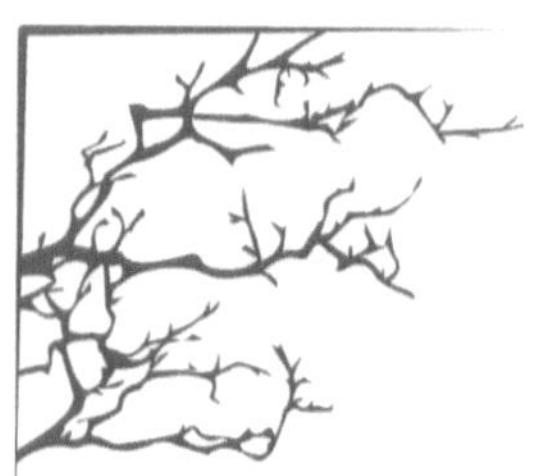

Chapter 12

The Council of Perth

We had arrived at West Dock. One of Sydney's suburbs in the West of Sydney. We approached a big man with full body armour and a sword the size of a tree and probably as heavy. He yelled "stop, monsieur. I have very strict orders from High Spell Crab to check all carts coming into this suburb. Once I'm done for the night, I can have a relaxing bubble bath and go to sleep in my nice comfy bed. Now, sir... can you please remove your bandanna. I need to see your face to check that you're not a darkened angel or a cursed". He lowered his bandanna to see a patch on his cheek. He asked "can you please remove the patch. And... Kyle, please check the back of the cart for the heirs to the seat thing". Maggi was hiding in a sack of potatoes. Kyle came in. he asked "are any of you the heirs to the council? I just have to check. You, there kid... you kind of look like this Ethos kid. Ethos is an angelic name. weird right?". I replied "I'm not Ethos, I'm Jack Big-Bottom. Bb for short". Kyle replied "my partner and I have to confirm your identity. The higher ups thought it was a bad Idea for us to date because we work together. Can you believe it? Sorry, rambling on about myself. Identification please". Ava very politely told him "we were attacked by a cursed on the way here. All our money, I.d and pretty much everything belonging the merchant that we are riding with apart from vegies and live-stock got stolen". Kyle replied, "I am so sorry, but I need some kind of proof". I showed him a wound I had gained from an angelic guard's spell. A scar on my shoulder. I replied "it has only just started to heal. The cursed mage took everything. I prayed and prayed that this guard didn't know much about magic. A cursed spell leaves a very different mark to a born spell". He replied "you're free to go. I'm so sorry for your loss". Up in front the large guard asked can I see what is under the patch?". Fatso replied "sorry, Dr's orders. An angel scratched me cheek in a little scuffle. The patch contains anti-bacterial agents. The nurse said it could get infected if I remove it and I might not be able to get it back on. It will likely start bleeding". The guard replied "let me refer you to a healer. She is quite mystically powerful and will have that scratch fixed in a jiffy". We rode by and found an inn. Ava sighed with amazing relief "Ahhh, they have beds. Nice comfy cosy beds". I replied, "I'm sleeping on the floor". Maggi replied "that's just as well. There are only 2 beds and I don't want to share mine with my brother". I asked "I'm just going to discuss the elephant in the room. How the hell are we going to get from Sydney to Perth if we can't fly or teleport?". Maggi replied "easy, the river of Evaneer. Sir Sheamus Evaneer was one of the first settlers in Australia. He decided that humans need a way to get from city to city. He used powerful beams of energy and a sail boat to carve the earth to make a stream surrounding Sydney. Once he was done, he thrust his magic from Sydney, to Canberra, to Melbourne, to Adelaide, to Darwin, to Perth, to Brisbane and back to Adelaide. Creating the greatest river in all of Australian history. It took him three years and an extremely powerful collection of borrowed artefacts, but he did it. We can use that river to go from Sydney, to Canberra, to Melbourne, to Adelaide, to Perth. All we need to do is catch a ride on a boat from Sydney to Perth". We went to sleep. I had a really weird dream. I found myself in the council room in Perth. Council member Morgan, council member Del Bar and my sister, the newly appointed Council member Ria were all sitting in the dining room. Council member Del Bar spoke "we all know why you called us here council member Reeper. You want to do the same thing your new age family has been trying to do for three generations. Not including yours yet of course. You want to make it legal for cursed to walk among us. Stop with this nonsense Miss Reeper. We won't change our minds". Ria replied "the force's of the Adelaide have a great advantage over us. Most of the human kingdoms can only use borrowed magic, like most of the angels can only use born magic. But Adelaide can use cursed magic. Cursed magic has a number of advantages. For one, cursed beings can have physical abilities that not even angels can rival. Also cursed magic can destroy borrowed artefacts which borrowed power can't do. In addition, cursed can use magic even if the artefact was knocked out of there hand". Council member Del Bar queried "I see your point Reeper. But I think there is a solution that will keep the towns people happy and still follow your argument. Two words, cursed conscription. We force cursed to fight for us".

A girl crept behind me. I knew her. She was a magic student studying In Perth Castle. I kind of have a crush on her. Her name is Emily. She asked "Ethos, what are you doing here? Only a borrowed Mage can use phantom vision". I queried "umm, what is phantom vision?". She replied "phantom vision is a power borrowed mages have that allows us to project our spirit into another place. But you're not a mage". I said, "am now".

Ria queried "do you have a death wish, council member Bar? Ever hear the fairy-tales where the cursed get revenge on the king? I can name at least 7". Council member Morgan replied in a rusty voice "may I intervene. If it is one vote for cursed being allowed in Perth and one for using them for military applications, I must side with the newer but wiser council member Ria". Del Bar yelled "council member Niff (Morgan's last name) please. Our proud clans have stood united against the cursed since the rise of humanity. Please, I implore you. Do not do this. Think of our heritage, our history". Morgan replied "I would rather have a human gut me with a knife than a werewolf eat me alive, Council Member Bar. I think that our descendants will likely agree with Ria. I want to be on the good side of history and remembered for being a progressive council member. The history books will not tarnish my name if I have anything to say about it".

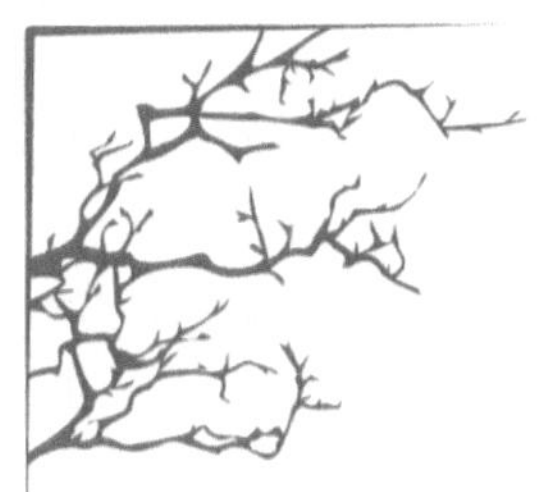

Chapter 13

Crab the Darkened Human

Ava was screaming in the night when I awoke. She screamed "don't kill her. No, no. You can't, I won't let you. NOOO". She awoke with a scream. I queried "nightmares again?". She replied "yeah". I heard a voice. It said "Ethos, Ethos... down here". I looked at my artefact. I saw Lucky's face in it. It said "hi Ethos. I put my hair in this artefact. I'm only about 1 full moon old. The point is that Crab's men have tracked us to this place. You need to get out of here but don't use the door. They are all on the other side". I woke Ava and Maggi. Ava asked "how do you know they are on the other side? Did you hear them?". I answered "let's go with that for now. But we need to get out of here". Ava whispered "what kind of man is Crab? And why do they call him Crab?". Maggi answered "his primary borrowed artefact comes from a Western Ghost Crabs claw. So, named because ghost crabs can appear and disappear at will. He has the same ability giving him his name. He holds an old belief that the magical are superior. He kept that belief hidden from Thunder for 5 years. He's very good at putting on a face when he needs to. He puts on a face for the council members. He refuses to take orders from the non-magical. Jane being his sister see's right through his facade. One more thing, he's Lucky's father". A man yelled from the other side of the door "Nathan, Kelly, break down the door. The door exploded. Crab yelled "secure the Angel. Kids come with me. I'm taking you back to Perth. I don't care what you want". I screamed "I'm not going anywhere with you". He bellowed "I don't think you non magical scum get a choice". I screamed as he walked in the door "I summon frost" and the floor froze over. Crab tripped. Ava opened the balcony. I jumped out and yelled "bubble of the night" and I thrust a bubble underneath me. Ava and Maggi jumped as well. Crab yelled "find them, now". Ava queried "why didn't he put on a face for you?". I answered, "because we saw right through it long ago". Crab screamed "claw of calamity". And he smashed the ice. Kelly asked "Crab, I thought you said he was non magical? How did he...". Crab replied "he didn't, he has the shield on his birth sign. There is no way he could have. That means either mental manipulation, or he's being possessed". A guard asked "if I may sir?....." Crab said this next part like it was a fact. Not in aggression or volume like a movie villain but simple and cold. "you may not, mages are hired to think. Guards are hired to fight". You should have seen the resentment in the sword woman's eyes. She had trained day and night for years to get on the Perth guard. Even then it took 12 months to get where she is now. And she had no choice but to listen to a being that thought her lesser. He screamed "guards with me, mages... hunt. But don't leave any wounds, my sister will never let me hear the end of it". Meanwhile we were running for our lives. Well Ava was running for her life. We were running from our child-hood fear. That is a pretty primal motivator too. We ran and hid for a long while. Eventually morning came but they knew we were in here. So, we decided to get creative. I replied, "I have a plan". Ava asked, "it better be better that running away from these guys all night". I approached a clothing store. I replied as we walked around the back "I know from experience that shops like this throw out stock all the time. If a dress doesn't sell, they chuck it. So, there are lots of perfectly good clothes out the back". Ava replied, "it's going to take a lot more than some new clothes to trick these guards". I replied "not changing clothes" as I grabbed a leather jacket and a pair of jeans and past them to Ava "switch genders. Failing that we'll just switch cloths". I grabbed a dress and a girl's hooded shirt. "Ava replied "you can't be serious". Voices of guards bellowed around the town. "split up and find them" they bellowed. Maggi replied, "classic mistake, telling the people your trying to find exactly where you are". I explained "Ava, the humans will be looking for an angel, a scrawny boy and a little girl. They won't be looking for a teenage boy, his girlfriend and a younger male child". Ava replied "yeah but, female angels are 7 times as strong as males. I've seen my brother Tom get trapped in my sister Nancy's pocket for 3 weeks. It traumatised me". Maggi calmed "it's ok, I promise you'll come out of this". She reluctantly put the jacket and pants on. We walked out of the ally and to the docks. Ava Asked, "why are we at the river again?". Maggi replied "because simple tracking spells can't track someone across running water. I thought they would have taught you that, being an angel and all". Ava explained "yeah, I don't really pay too much attention to that kind of stuff". I chanted "bubble of the night" and I thrust my hand from my mouth outward launching a bubble into the water". Ava queried "why can't I just fly you across?". Maggi replied, "good point". A young woman with a blind fold approached us. It was clear she was blind. She replied "if you're going west my uncle is headed that way to visit my sister. She won an award from Perth Castles magic program. We are headed there across the Evaneer River". I replied, "that is exactly where we're going". She asked, "why are you wearing a dress?". I lied "I lost a bet. if you're blind, how do you know?". She replied, "I have other senses you know". she approached her uncle. He asked "who are these people? Do they need a lift?". Maggi replied, "I'm afraid so". I had taken off the dress at that point. He asked "I'm afraid I can't let people on board. Not with this kind of tension in the air. Cursed are everywhere. And for all I know you're angels. My niece really should stop dating angels". She replied "2 angels, 2. I have had a total of 5 boyfriends, 2 were angels. I'm 17 Mike, not 12". He laughed "well, your boyfriend aint coming on board. I have valuable cargo. I have to get this sugar to Perth". I replied "I can pay you. I have human Australian money on me. I could give you 50". The man replied "very well, come aboard. But I must warn you, there are water-maidens in this river. Powerful creatures. Like water they can be solid liquid or gas. They're freezing crystal when they're solid. Men are rare in their society.

They need humans to travel long distances out of water. Even before borrowed power was possible, they had a sport. They have this game to see who can get the most humans underwater in the shortest time. They can even take angels under water". I replied as we walked onto his ship "don't have to tell me. I've been possessed once".

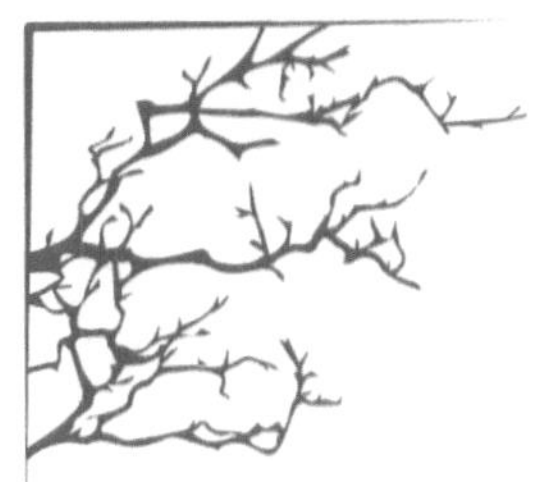

Chapter 14

What is Rellik Spelt Backwards

Rellik was back in his tower. He sat in the Prince's seat. An elf approached him. He walked through the door and yelled "tell me where my sister is idiot. Or I'll wipe this earth clean of you". Rellik asked "you could be a bit more polite. You may be non-magical but that doesn't mean we can't be friends. Did you bring it, Elf?". He replied "I did. This bracelet will allow you to fight the binding stopping you from attacking the few people protected by the Key of Harmony. I do this under protest to save my sister I will do anything. Let me warn you, this artefact will allow you to fight the binding not over come it". Rellik yelled "not good enough, elf. You want your sister, overcome my plight. Don't let me fight it. Friends don't do that". The Elf yelled "I can assure you this is the best you will get from anyone. You could spend a year crafting a solution and you would end up with something less effective. I promise you angel, you have made an enemy, while the young council members have made an ally. Rellik spoke "fine, have your sister back". He grabbed a bag from inside his seat. "she was getting feisty anyway. Cut me on the shoulder". He threw the human size bag with a person in it at the elf. He sliced the ropes of his sister's bag. He gave his sister a wand and she got up. She ordered "I am Eia Fright and I swear to you, I will protect Ava, Ethos and Maggi. You have allied the council of Perth with me". The male Elf threw the bracelet on the floor and walked out. Rellik queried "that's it? Run to your fellow non magical beings. You have doomed two humans". The male elf named Draco Fright proclaimed "you don't have the will to over come it anyway. Even with that artefact".

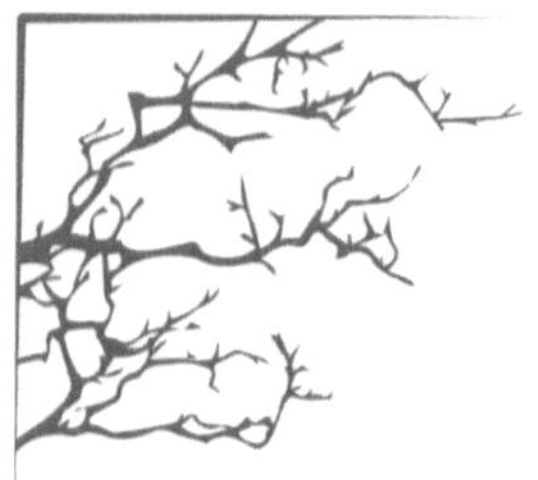

Chapter 15

Water Maidens

The sun arose that frosty winter morning. This girl's uncle had called me to the bridge. He replied as light rain blossomed making ripples in the water "you are the leader of your group, so I'll address this warning to you. There's a storm coming. Both metaphorically and literally. The clouds are gathering in weird formations. Formations that bring up painful memories. There's a storm on the horizon, its written in the sky. But there is also a storm coming for all of humanity. The angels will descend from the sky in a wall of fire and lightning. Borrowed power will be hurled from earth to the sky as the descending life forms sing their song of death. Hard times are ahead my boy. For everyone". He looked in my jacket pocket. He saw... my borrowed artefact. He replied, "do you be a borrowed mage or just someone who killed one for their stone?". I answered "my artefact is my own. And I am a borrowed caster. Only I just figured it out literally 2 days ago. I have no idea what I'm doing". He replied "maybe my niece can teach yah a thing or two. She is obsessed with magic but for some reason her mother doesn't think shell be safe at Perth Castle although we have family ties there. Let me tell yah, I don't mean to brag, but I am this close to having a family relation inside the Reeper family. My other niece, Emily Shade, she has a crush on that Reeper boy". I spat "you shouldn't talk about your niece that way. That is a private matter she trusted you with and you betrayed that trust. And to brag to some one you only met that day no less". I walked out of the room. He yelled out to me "if you told me ye were a borrowed mage I would have let you and your friends on board sooner. I was just worried you were angels". I continued to walk away with my arm's crossed. Meanwhile down below deck Maggi and Ava were talking to the girl we met on the docks. Her name was Quoa. Quoa queried "let me guess, you are Maggi and Ethos the heirs to the Council of Perth. Ava is 9th in line out of 12 heirs to the western angelic throne. Did I guess right?". Ava stammered "how the hell did you know?". Maggi answered "because of her curse. You mentioned you're blind so I'm guessing you're one of the few living inheritors of the blind book curse. It trades the ability to see for literally all written knowledge. That is how you know who we are". She yelled "don't tell my uncle. Am I clear? I can do magic despite being self-taught and I am more than capable of destroying an angelic princess". Ava spat out these words with a righteous simple vindictive tone "don't call me princess. Clear". She replied "I don't only know of your status, but I know of your uncle, your scar and all your mother's secrets she kept from you. Unfortunately, you're not emotionally ready to hear them yet". Ava asked "what do you mean... my mother's secret? What has she kept from me?". Quoa replied "what you think you did at first may not be the truth. The black cat doesn't have the whole story. Only the true culprit and you have that information". Maggi replied, "what the magic was that?". Quoa responded "I can't tell you the whole story until you're emotionally ready. I'm sorry but the truth can break those who hear it to soon".

I walked in the door. 8 minutes later a man stepped out of nowhere. He threatened "you thought you could hide from me. I will have you two back in Perth in a jiffy. Maggi growled "we are doing fine on our own thanks. A voice came over the intercom. Attention passengers, we are entering Water Maiden territory". "Brace yourself" Quoa said. As Crab readied to attack Ava with an attack of devastating light, water crept into the cabin. The attack shot at Ava but curved around knocking the borrowed artefact out of my hand. I grabbed a sword. What Crab tragically failed to realise was that the water around his feet was a spell casting water maiden. She materialised as a woman made of ice and pulled Crab under water. Thankfully as Mike explained the water maidens have very creative ways of keeping the human's they drag underwater alive. She literally pulled him through the wooden deck without penetrating it. Like a ghost. I made a lunge for the borrowed artefact and grabbed it. Ava ordered "listen to me Ethos, protect the borrowed artefact. Stand on your side, use your leg to protect the artefact and point the other hand outward facing your enemy. In angel school, they always taught us to attack the borrowed artefact. A magical creature will always attack the borrowed artefact". I did as she said. After that a puddle flowed down the stairs and became a young woman made of ice. She said "sorry, but I'm playing a game. The loser has to get pushed down the sink". The young lady turned into steam as another came through the window. I yelled "I summon frost "and the gas cloud froze back into the woman. A boy this time came in through the window in a watery humanoid shape. He was with 6 women. Three of them had a seaweed cross inside of their water form and the others had a shell. Probably to tell what team they're on. I muttered "I summon frost" and froze the 7 of them. One said "I can't use my water or steam form. What kind of magic is this?". Maggi replied "it's a simple frost spell. A very common spell". The crazy uncle announced over the intercom "we are about to enter the final stretch to the dock. There, we will pick up supplies, and head straight to Adelaide non-stop. My sister has a much faster boat than this one that can get us there much quicker". "BOOM" the boat rocked with thunderous power. Ava replied "nope, I know that sound too well. Its an angelic attack". BOOM "and from the sound of it, there's a lot of them". One of the young women asked, "what are we going to do?". Maggi replied "I'll tell you, we have to work together. You 5 water girls, take as many angels as you can under water. You three and Ethos, you're all Mages. Give us some cover fire. The rest of you, we keep this boat working. We man the sails, keep all non-living water out and give more cover fire with the ballistae. We'll give those angel's a run for their money". I replied "see what I mean? You would be a great council member. You should totally get the seat on the Perth Council. Maggi yelled "not while we're under attack". I responded, "yes Council Member Maggi". I went above deck. The main sail had more holes than a sponge and was on fire. I yelled into the sky *"I summon frost"* and powerful icy magic erupted into the sky. Thunder and rain poured down onto the boat. It was only a matter of time before they breached the hull. I saw two Angels charging the control tower. That was where Mike was. One angel readied a lightning bolt while the other readied a curse. I heard one say "I curse you to be a dog. Sit boy". Maggi yelled to Quoa, "that angel is going to curse your uncle". I jumped in between the lightning and Mike and proclaimed, "bubble of the night" and the bubble rushed forward popping after making contact with the lightning. The bubble had stopped the spell, but Mike was still cursed. He yelled "why didn't you stop the curse instead of the lightning boy. If I had have got hit with lightening, I would have lost an arm or leg. I might have got a scar but a curse, I lose everything. My humanity, my life, my dignity, my freedom. I become lesser. Don't you understand... boy". I replied "you're being ridiculous. You just hate cursed because you don't know one well enough to feel for them". He yelled "I have no home now. No one will love me". I screamed "try Adelaide genius. Not all humans are total Jerks to cursed". He yelled "undo my curse. Please, I beg of you almighty master of spells. Undo my horrible curse". I said these next two words like I was talking to a toddler "I just told you I learnt magic a few nights ago. To undo the werewolf curse I would need to be a high mage. The grades go student mage, graduate mage, low mage, medium mage, high mage, master mage and lord mage. I'm not even a student yet". I grabbed a ballista on the bridge. It was designed to fend of attacks from sea monsters. I was trying something I never tried before "spirits of the wild" I chanted rubbing the arrow trying to channel magic into it "hunt the angry angels". The arrow glowed white and I fired it. It shot into the sky exploding at one angels shield. The angry spirits of Birds of Prey and slithering snakes rushed at the flying humanoids. I screamed into the water, we can swim to shore and lose them in the forest.

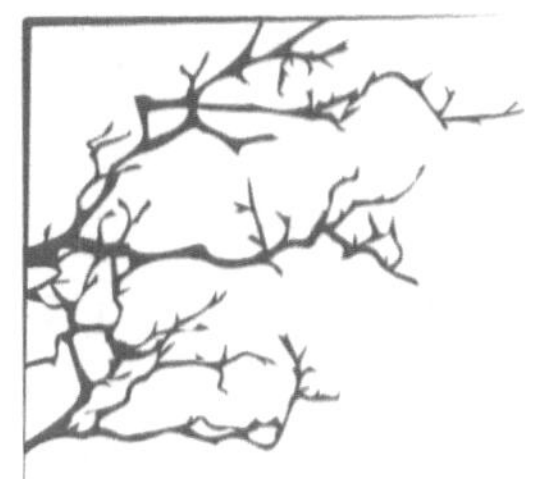

Chapter 15

The Flood

Yesterday Rellik's mother yelled at him for what he had done to the Elves. "I know you like to plunder non magical beings and I have been very lenient about that. But the Southern Elves are in revolt. You took dozens of them captive without my permission or the permission of the council. And as a result, they are demanding we turn you over to them". Rellik replied "relax mum, we can wipe them out no problem". Relliks mum roared "some of us have an objection to genocide. Elves are not only elite archers but they attach borrowed artefact's into their bows allowing them to shoot beams of both physical and arcane hitting dozens of targets at once. We'll be lucky if they only assassinate you. They're likely to come after our whole family. Bloody magic, we'll be lucky if they take the whole family hostage. We will be especially lucky if they demand our family steps down from angelic lordship". Rellik responded "they're not protected by the Key of Harmony. I don't see a problem". "I am Gia Rose, you will listen to me Rellik Gia. You are very lucky I don't use you as a peace offering. They said if we gave you up to them for a fair trial, they would leave us alone. But you will do as I say. Assassinate Ethos and Maggi Reeper. We can't even touch the Perth kingdom, as long as the Reepers are in charge, thanks to the Key of Harmony. If those two get back to Perth we won't be able to touch their army's and the elves will surely be helping them. After that you will proceed directly to Perth and assassinate Ria Reeper leaving Perth open to a pre-emptive strike. I hereby revoke your right to the throne. I don't care if you're the oldest of four, I will not have a murderer ruling the south". Rellik gave in "yes, Lord Gia".

Back in the present Mike replied "there's no point in them running after all of us as a group. If we split up, they have to split up. I'll go with Quoa you three meet us at the Sydney Evaneer docks". Ava replied "good for you. You're finally getting over being cursed". Mike yelled "I am far from over it. I am an abomination and always will be". We bolted, but back at the river something was happening. Rellik approached the angels. He proclaimed "don't go in there and hunt them. That's way too fair. Flood the forest and let them drown". One of the angels replied "that's not actually a bad idea. Let's do it guys". They all focused their minds and the water rushed into the forest. Minutes later we saw the impending tide. I yelled "I have a plan. Bubble of the night". I jumped in the bubble and motioned "come on in. quickly". Ava bellowed "its too thin". I screamed "NO TIME". They hopped in the bubble. I yelled "I summon frost" and the bubble froze over. The bubble became a chunk of ice 6 meters think. The water smashed into the bubble. I saw an orange light outside the bubble. It said "you are no match for Crab. He is a master mage. I know you're not possessed. So how did Ethos learn magic? The boy with the mysterious prophecy. The tower, the shield and yin and yang". I told the light "I guess they lied to both of us... Master Mage Humphrey". The voice screamed "how dare you. I am fiercely loyal to Crab and NO ONE calls him that". A purple light replied "I'm not, I'm his back up artefact. I'm made from water-maiden hair. The Crab artefact is weak to smoke and heat". The Crab artefact yelled "don't tell him that". The water maiden Borrowed Artefact said "I want out of this malicious monsters' clutches. Ethos is a capable Mage. I will be passed on down the family line whether Humphrey likes it or not". Ava asked "um, who are you talking to?". I replied "I'm not really sure. My best guess, Crabs borrowed artefacts". Maggi yelled "are you sure? Not just anyone can speak to the borrowed". Ava asked "why is this such a big deal?...". Maggi interrupted sharply "you're an angel. I was under the impression that angelic parents taught their kids about certain types of mages to be very cautious of. I thought borrowed whisperers were on the top end of the list". Ava replied, "they probably did but I don't tend to pay much attention". Maggi bellowed "borrowed whispering is only gifted to the Spell Casters with mountains of potential. The power is half-way between born and cursed magic. If a borrowed whisperer gets their hands on a borrowed artefact you have possessed at any point in your life they can know all of your secrets in a matter of minutes. They have options that other mages can only dream of and can learn spells directly from borrowed artefacts. Some of these artefacts know spells not accessible any other way. Some spells are even lost for centuries". Ava responded, "well I'm glad he's on my side and not against me". I responded "I don't really know how to respond. Do I get scared of that power, do I get excited that I have these options? I really don't know".

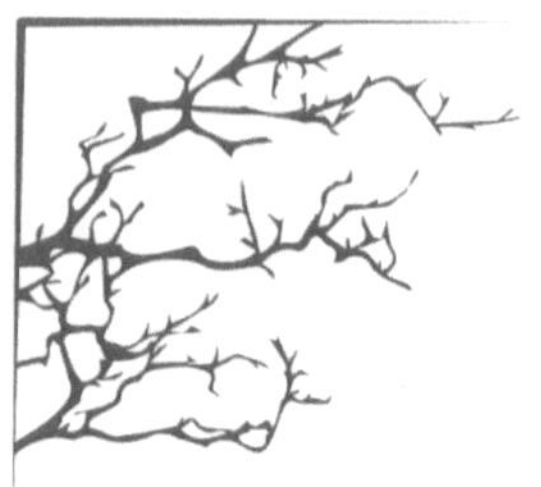

Chapter 16

Parramatta

The flood eventually ended at Parramatta. The last suburb before the before Sydney's Kingdom turns into the wilds of Australia. Filled with mystical creatures thousands of which are undiscovered. Thousands more can be found nowhere else on earth. For this reason, Parramatta has one of the strongest military forces in all of Sydney. The towns on the edge of the border have more weaponry than anywhere else. Because they are more dangerous than anywhere else. It was also home to the Sydney Evaneer docks. From the top of the hill where we stood there was an amazing view. You could see a river flow across like a moat protecting all of Sydney. You could also see a river stretching out south-west. The town was spectacular. There were guard towers, lamington stands, catapults and a massive park. You could even see the docks from the hill. We snuck into town only to find a worried crowd. Ava asked one of them "excuse me ma'am, what is everyone so scared of?". The elderly woman replied "there's a storm coming. A bad one. Magic has always been strong near the border, even stronger across Evaneer river. We have a lot of magical people in our population. But we grow worried. The storm could be an invitation, a distraction from everything that lurks across that line. If you're living on the border it is wise to be afraid. Very wise". We wandered past her. Maggi replied "don't worry, the sky looks fine". I stammered "no, its not fine. The creepy old man on the ship told me to beware of a storm". Ava explained "he's right, angels are taught to sense very slight changes in pressure from a young age. I can feel it, I can feel the storm coming". Maggi ordered "sit down, you clearly don't know anything about magic so I'm going to teach you". Ava queried "how do you know so much? I thought you would be taught strategy, history, leadership and sword play like most heirs to the council. Not magic". Maggi responded "I kind of spy on magic classes in my spare time. I also read about magic from books in the library. I would give anything to be a magic student. Although I know the entire curriculum off by heart, I really want my graduate mage certificate. Now, magic 101. Magic is the art of manipulating science to transform matter and energy. To manipulate science, you need life essence. The most raw, primal and ancient type of magic. Life essence is different depending on what direction you're born in. Humans and other non-magic animals have life essence but it is balanced between north, east, south and west or magically neutral. In magical bodies one direction is more powerful than the others. This makes them magically charged. Borrowed artefacts are a bit more complicated. Centuries before borrowed magic existed angels used gemstones to channel their power. The magic flows through the crystal from the magically charged object and into the nearest magically neutral object. In this case, a human". We found a hotel nearby. It was named "the Evaneer Inn" and had direct access to the Sydney docks. Maggi paid 30 human dollars for the night. As we went to the room, we saw a familiar face. A face that had a black cat birth mark on her cheek. She had black hair running down her back and wore all black. Black pants and a black singlet with a borrowed bracelet, necklace, ring, belt and crystal skull. She had amber eyes and pink skin. It was Lucky. She had a look of remorse on her face. I asked "Lucky, are you ok?". She stopped me "I don't deserve that. In my grief I attacked both of you, put Ava's life in danger although it wasn't her fault and I lost control". Ava replied "your allowed to lose control once in a while. Everyone does it". Lucky interrupted "not mages. Mages aren't allowed to lose control. If we even mis-aim, or mispronounce a spell some once could die. I attacked you. I wanted to hurt you, make you suffer. I will never forgive myself for that. In that moment I became my father. Someone I swore I would never be". A tear trickled down her face. I saw a terrible orange glow behind Lucky. I bellowed "speaking of your father" I grabbed a sword "LOOK OUT" and I struck the orange artefact. Crab fell to the ground. I asked Lucky "do you know any smoke spells? Or heat spells?". Lucky replied "several, why?". Crab got to his feet but Lucky bellowed "dad, if you so much as touch a hair on their head's I swear to magic I will name you". Crab stammered "you wouldn't. I'm just trying to return my dear nephews' home safely. Don't make me choose between my life and helping my family". Maggi replied "and cue the face. From monster to monster in a human mask". Lucky spat "you don't want to help them. You want to be the hero that takes them back to safety. The council of Perth said if you do that, they'll consider you for a Lord Mage certificate. Putting you on even ground with my mother". He stammered with fake fear in his voice "please, don't do this. I am your father. I gave you life. We share blood". She ordered "go to your room". He walked into his room. Thunder clapped in the distance. Ava stated "we're stuck in here until the storm clears. Its going to be a long night".

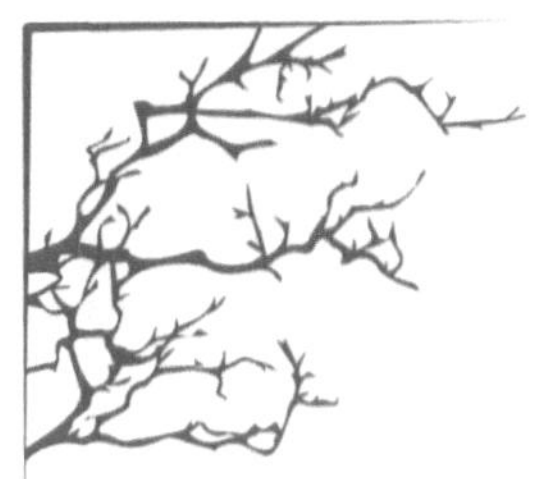

Chapter 17

The Evaneer Inn

The time was 4:30AM on a Monday morning. A storm was raging outside. I was awake reading the book Fatso had stolen. It had lots and lots of magic. Ancient magic. I even found a spell that can turn a human into an Angel. Lucky woke up and saw Ava yelling out in the night. "Show yourself, I know you're there. No, you can't have my memory". Ava grasped her temples screaming in horror. "AHHHH AHHH. GET OUT OF MY HEAD. GET OUT OF MY MIND. YOU WON'T OVERTAKE ME I WON'T LET YOU IN. I am Sleepless Angel Ava. AAAHHHHHH". Ava awoke. She asked lucky "I need to know. What exactly did I do? What on earth could I have done to make you that mad. I'm sorry whatever I did but I need to know". Lucky confessed "I think you know. You killed council member Jane". Ava stammered "I don't care that I killed a council member nearly as much as the fact I killed their mother". Lucky said "I was given a task to bring her back. But if anyone should be apologising, its me. I wanted to kill you back there. I called you a Darkened Angel when in that moment, I was a Darkened Human". Ava queried "did you ever imagine that Ethos would be a mage?". Footsteps sounded down the hall. Lucky stammered "Ethos couldn't be a spell caster. He has a shield in his birth prophecy". Ava replied "he is a mage. He has been using that borrowed thingy he took from you this whole time". Lucky sighed "son of a *%$#@. They lied to him about his birth prophecy. They lied to me about his birth prophecy. Sure, I tried that thing out, but I didn't expect it to work". Ava asked, "what thing didn't you expect to work?". Lucky answered "there are cheat codes to becoming a spell caster. The most common and probably most detrimental ones is implanting the memories of another magic user in to your mind. Its quick, its easy, it's a crime against nature. But I read about a less known cheat code, an ancient one. As old as borrowed power itself. If you know a magical creature well enough using a borrowed artefact containing their DNA is second nature. You know them, you know their power. I thought I would test it out on Ethos, but it was such an obscure technique I didn't expect it to work". Ava questioned "maybe he just defied his prophecy. I know for a fact that prophecies can be defied". Lucky replied "maybe, but parents lie to kids about there prophecy a lot. More than half the time. People defy prophecies 5 maybe 10 percent of the time. And a mortal weapon in a prophecy is as solid of an indicator as they get". I heard an artefact say on the other side of the door "my mistress will destroy you with this spell young mage". I heard "fog of thunder, fog of sleep, use the power which I keep. Spread by will, spread by light, take away their will to fight. From my mist we make them sleep, dawn of the night to make them weep". Fog rolled under the door. I yelled "Maggi, wake up, that is no ordinary mist. Quickly out the window".

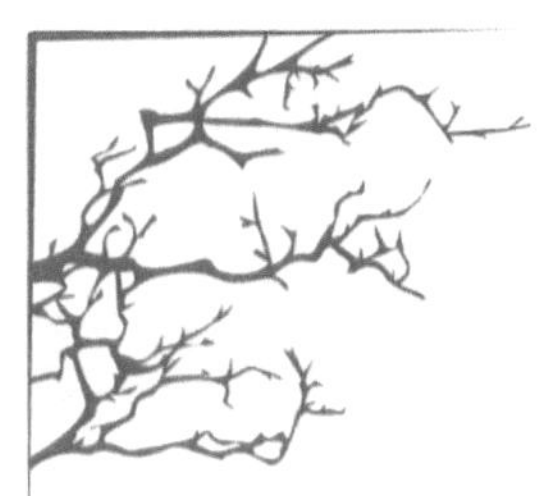

Chapter 18

The Lightning Struck Bell Tower

Maggi got up and yelled "what is that mist? What is going on?". Lucky answered "that is mind fog. It's a new age spell that generates a mist that makes you sleep. You can only be woken by the person that put you to sleep or after the fog clears. Ethos is right, we need to climb out the window. I would sooner take my chances with the storm than that fog". Ava replied "I think our best option is to climb over the Inn and get to a boat. The fog won't be able to cross the water". We all climbed out the window. The dark of night and the raging winds made it easy to stay focussed. Ava replied "we can travel around the inn and through the park. It's the safest way". Crab replied "you're not going anywhere kiddies. Not with this storm you're not". I stammered as Crab made a wall of fire boxing us in "climb to the second story. I summon frost". The water from the storm froze making a ladder. We climbed and climbed up the frosty rungs. They were slippery and cold but not impossible to climb. We grasped onto the second story. Ava ordered "quickly, run to the other side of the Inn. There's not much time". We got about half-way there when Rellik appeared blocking our way. He said "guess who? That's right, it's the human killer". Ava got her scythe out and yelled "I've been waiting years to do this. Rellik, you've met your match". The mind fog crept up the stairs. Going forward was no longer an option. Rellik yelled as he blocked Ava's strike "I am immune to the fog. And as long as I hold... this" Rellik held up an enchanted river stone. "the fog can't touch me". Lucky yelled "you can't make the fog. You don't have magic, let alone that kind of magic". Maggi stammered "unless, it wasn't him". I saw a spiralling stair case down the hall. I commanded "this way, I have an idea". We bolted up the stairs. We found ourselves in a bell tower. Lucky queried "can anyone translate this writing?". Maggi looked at it and replied "it is ancient borrowed language. Not easily translatable but is says Evaneer lives within these walls. The 8 Cities have 8 Inns. Each connected by the great river. Within the Inns, lays Evaneers soul. They Project his spirit into the water". Lucky jumped "I get it, there are 8 Inns for 8 capital city's which project his soul into the river". Rellik walked up onto the stairs along with a young borrowed mage. It was Kelly, the student mage who broke down the door of the last Inn they were in. The one working with Crab". Crab appeared from thin air on the roof top. Kelly explained "I'm sorry guys, but he gave me his feather for a borrowed artefact. That will be invaluable. The feather of an heir to the Southern Angelic Throne". Maggi yelled "HOW COULD YOU!". Rellik tried to shoot a bow at me but his hand jerked to the side. He tried again aiming at Maggi but it hit the bell making it ding. Crab screamed "I was going to make you my apprentice, girl. How could you do that?". Kelly replied As Rellik focussed his will to overcome the binding. Kelly replied "I know there's nothing I can do to make it up to you. Except perhaps... "I name Rellik Gia by his feather". The feather burst into flames. It used itself to make Rellik collapse in front of us". Crab proclaimed "very well played Kelly. You will make a fine apprentice. Now, use the mind fog on the kids". Kelly shot the mind fog at Crab. He passed out. She then dissipated the fog while still keeping Crab asleep. She hugged me and said "I'm sorry I had to do that. But it was necessary to win that battle. I'll see you if the will of the borrowed wants it to be". She walked down the stairs. The purple artefact yelled at me "what are you waiting for Ethos, grab me". I did. But then I realised "the diary Fatso stole. She took it". She was halfway down the hall. I yelled guided by the purple borrowed artefact "LIGHTNING I CALL YOU FORTH" and lightning flowed down from the clouds and hit the stone tower inside the Inn. The lightning flowed through the stone tower and down into the IInn. It electrified the floor for half a second. Half a second should have been enough. But when we went down to investigate, there was a note and a scorch mark on the carpet. It said, "try harder next time, and there will be a next time". Lucky shuddered with excitement "new villain alert...... Awesome".

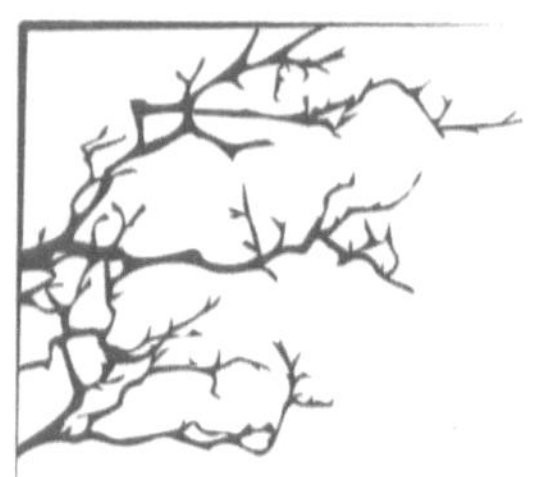

Chapter 19

Who Really Killed Jane?

The same Sleepless Angel that brainwashed Ava approached Rellik. She replied "you will do what I say human killer. I deeply regret my actions. You know, the whole... brainwashing Ava thing. I've realised that the Order of the Sleepless doesn't have the world's best interests at heart. I was misguided. But I need you to get something from the Reeper family. Something that will make the Key of Harmony work. Can you do that for me. Because I will heal you, and then I will give you a curse if you don't cooperate. A curse that will keep you from killing anyone. Am I clear, Rellik?". He muffled "do I have a choice?". She replied "nope".

Meanwhile we got onto a boat a mere hour after the storm ended. Quoa and her uncle took us aboard Quoas mothers ship. As it turned out they were on their mothers boat the whole time. Since there were only a few beds we slept on the decks. Ava was about to have her final and worst nightmare. Her dream started like most of the others. She was standing outside her body watching herself. In the castle pointing her borrowed artefact at Jane. Jane said, "oh it's you". She yelled "I will kill you Jane. You won't survive this". Jane took out her sword. Ghost Ava yelled "don't do it. You're better than this. You can fight it". Then she charged swinging her scythe countless times. Jane proclaimed "I won't do it again, I won't do it again, I won't do it again" over and over again. That was when Ava saw herself walk into the room. Jane just stared in confusion. The other Ava replied "I have been ordered to take care of this woman by the High Night Angel. Take care of the two heirs". Jane had a look of realisation on her face. She tried tried to yell but it came out as a whisper. You, you,

you're Fury. Ava's mother". Ava walked through the portrait hole. The second Ava was out of sight she drew up a powerful magical killing spell". Jane yelled "I won't kill again. Never again". A flash of bright blue light erupted through the hall. Fury still had Ava's appearance when Lucky walked down the hall. "how could you do this? Ok, focus, healing spells. Healing spells" she stammered as Jane lay bleeding on the ground. Ava awoke with a start. By far that was the worst nightmare of all. Quoa walked out in the still, quiet night while the moonlight covered them in its rays. She said "I told you what you thought you did at first may not be the truth. The black cat doesn't have the whole story. Only the true culprit and you have that information". Ava yelled out "it wasn't me, it wasn't me! Wait, it wasn't me! It was an Angelic Lord. Oh, crud it was an Angelic Lord".

by

William Stone Greenhill.
Dedicated to Oscar, my best frend

Don't miss out!

Visit the website below and you can sign up to receive emails whenever william stone greenhill publishes a new book. There's no charge and no obligation.

https://books2read.com/r/B-A-BLSJ-WMZCB

BOOKS2READ

Connecting independent readers to independent writers.

Did you love *Borrowed Magic*? Then you should read *Borrowed magic the Second*[1] by william stone greenhill!

[2]

In the old times magic ruled the world. I guess it still does in some ways but now humans have magic. Before humans had magic, people suffered, and angels ruled everything. Humans were suffering but innocent. Until a human found new magic. But that is an old story. The new story starts 900 years ago when the angels are debating what to do about the new human magic population. An Angelic Mage named Tye Lee was crafting a unique type of magic. Cursed magic. It attached a spell to a human permanently. Changing their biology. Their soul itself. Tye Lee channelled her new spell into a human King. She yelled "I curse you to be a dog. Sit... @#$%&". And despite his profanity's and screaming for guards, nothing happened. Until the full moon when he turned into a

---

1. https://books2read.com/u/3JD1Rv

2. https://books2read.com/u/3JD1Rv

beast like no other. An intelligent, hungry K9 out to destroy everything. That is until the moon fell. Impressed, they made Tye Lee a Lord Mage. And so, came a new method of keeping humans scared and weak. Until a human mage returned the favour. Angels thought themselves immune to such a power for magic dwelled within them. They thought very, very wrong. Humans developed specific curses that could be used on angels. With time the cursed became thought of as lesser beings. But a century ago, three members of the Reeper family had an idea. Cursed were being subjected not only to great injustice. But they were still powerful. The three Reeper sisters travelled the world gathering the hair of the most powerful cursed. They met back in Perth castle and placed the hair in a borrowed artefact made from crystal that fell from the heavens. One of the sisters became... The Cursed Lantern. The Cursed Lantern ran across Perth and helped cursed whenever and however they could. Under the light of the moon. It became one of the few bedtime stories that didn't paint cursed as the monsters as the sisters originally intended. In the present we look at the current user of the cursed lantern. Ethos Reeper. Just a week ago the entire of Australia gathered together to forge a binding contract that said they couldn't wage war on each other. It didn't work and a brawl ensued. Maggi (Ethos's sister) Ava (the daughter of an Angelic lord) and Ethos ran away to get back home.

About the Author

Hi, I'm William greenhill. I was born in Fremantle WA and I love writing stories. I am a massive nerd and I love it. I have autism and A.D.H.D and I'm darn proud of it. I always wanted to be in a fantasy world. I have always admired the hero's of stories. I always wanted to be one. But sadly that's not an option. So instead to get a fantasy fix I write stories. Lets face it, who wouldn't.

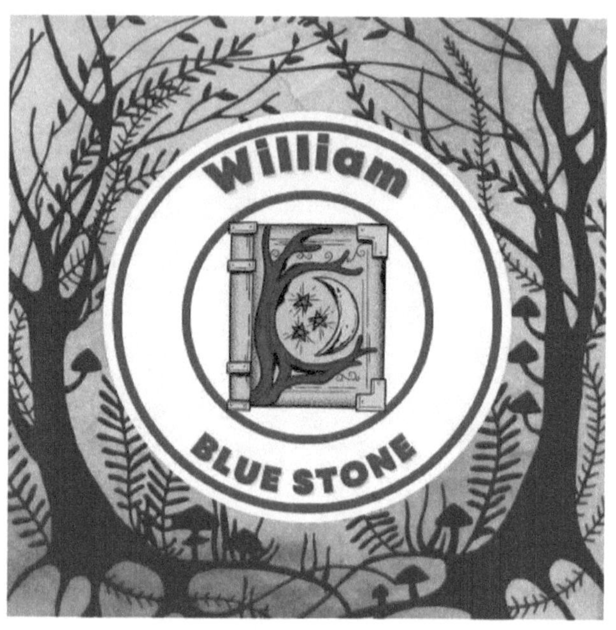

About the Publisher

Hi, I'm William greenhill. I was born in Fremantle WA and I love writing stories. I am a massive nerd and I love it. I have autism and A.D.H.D and I'm darn proud of it. I always wanted to be in a fantasy world. I have always admired the hero's of stories. I always wanted to be one. But sadly that's not an option. So instead to get a fantasy fix I write stories. Lets face it, who wouldn't.